Colin and Jacqui Hawkins

PictureLions
An Imprint of HarperCollinsPublishers

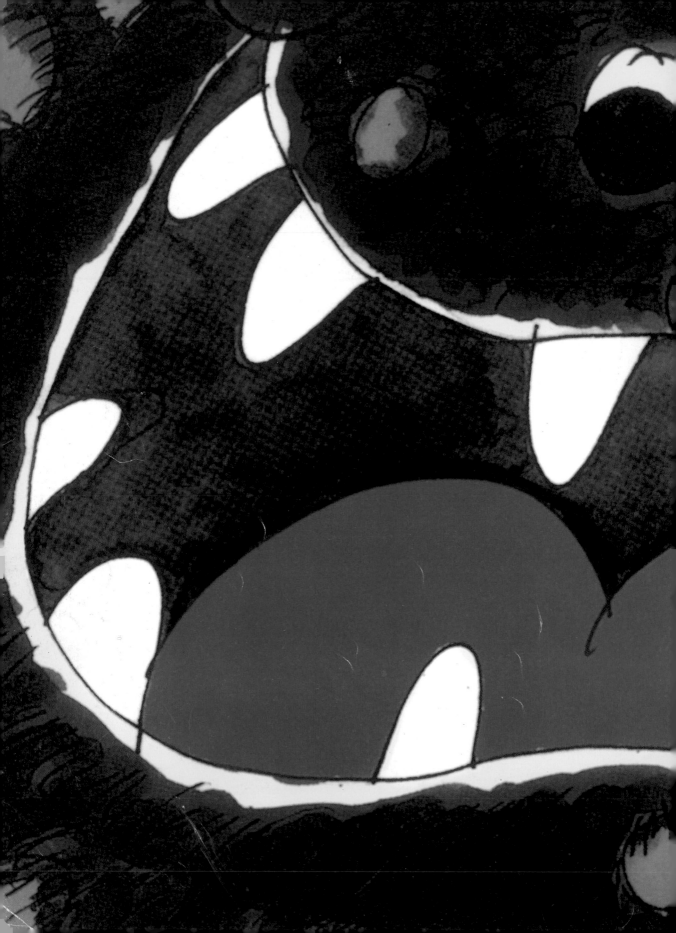

Beware the lonely road, beware the dark forest, beware the gloomy cave, for here lurks ... the beast; hairy of leg, hairy of face, foul of breath, shambling and loping of gait, sharp in tooth and claw, beware the creature of darkness!

A good description you might think of lots of things that go bump in the night, but this ancient text relates to creatures that are always described in hushed tones as gigantic, fearsome, dangerous and wicked. Sometimes green and slimy with long squirming tongues; sometimes soft and squidgy with four eyes, six legs, and spitting poison and sometimes coming from outer space: they are **MONSTERS!**
In this book we will explore the world of the monster. Who were they? Do they still exist? Where do they live? Do they have any friends? What and whom do they eat? Which are the worst monsters? Do you know a monster? All these and many more monstrous questions will be answered.

* Typical monster greeting.

Woodsman Lore:- All they monsters ave an 'airy belly. Their feet ave huge and 'orribly 'orribly smelly!

Hairy, Scary and BIG

Do you know of anyone with big hairy feet?

|← 30 inches (or 4 × the width of this page) →|

Huge hairy monsters with enormous feet live in the forests of Canada and America. They are called 'Big Foot' or 'Sasquatch' by the native Americans. In 1924 Albert Ostman was carried off by a Big Foot while he was camping, though luckily he managed to escape. He reported that the creature was about three metres tall, covered in reddish brown hair and had very big smelly feet.

In Tibet they call the hairy giant the 'Yeti' or 'Abominable Snowman'. It lives high up in the Himalayan mountains. ✳

The Australians call their monster the 'Yowie'.

Ranger lore:–

> *The Yowie likes a booze*
> *An' then he has a snooze.*

✳ You'd have to be sly to see a Yeti pass by
They live way up high and are very very shy.
(Old sherpa rhyme)

Howie Yowie!

Good on Ya Boo!

A werewolf* is a terrifying sight: have you seen a man transformed into a ferocious wolf every full moon? There are several signs by which a werewolf can be recognised. Take a good look around you. Do you see anyone with eyebrows that meet in the middle, with small pointed ears, sharp fingernails and, the surest sign of all, hairs on the palms of the hands?

Beware Werewolves

Are you weird enough to become a werewolf? If you are — there are various methods you can try.

It's working.

Roll in the sand at full moon.

Mmm.. Mmm..

Give me a bite.

Eat wolfbane sandwiches for packed lunch or supper.

Drink from the same water as a wolf.

(Perhaps you could let us know if any of these work.)

St Patrick cursed an Irish family who had upset him. They became werewolves every seven years for seventy years.

A curse on yee!

Grrrr! Grrr!

It was rumoured that King John was a werewolf. Norman monks heard sounds coming from his grave. They dug him up and re-buried him in unconsecrated ground.

?   ?

Wooooooooo! Wooooooooo!

King John was a hairy fellow, with teeth long and yellow. His breath was smelly and really foul and every night you'd hear him howl.

werewolves are hairy and very scary.

The werewolf can be defeated by taking three drops of its blood, while it is still in wolf form. An easier remedy is to shoot the wolf with a silver bullet. Or if you know his human name call it out loudly three times. Failing all these – RUN!

* Wer – Old english for man hence werewolf.

Sea Monsters

In all the seas of the world dwell terrible, tentacled, squirming sea monsters and slippery, spitting sea serpents. They are the terror and torment of all those who sail the seven seas.

One of the largest sea-serpents ever encountered met the Bishop of Uppsala in Sweden in 1555. He described it as a very big serpent indeed, at least sixty metres in length and some six metres round with a mane of red hair.*

In November 1861, the crew of the French ship Electon battled with a huge sea creature. The monster eventually made off leaving behind an eight metre length of its tail.

*Possibly Scottish or Viking serpent.

How do you suppose
when a serpent grows
He tickles his toes
and picks his nose?
No one knows.

In the dark and gloomy mist a sea serpent hissed...

I've just eaten up my brother, Now I'll go and eat up mother.

Old mariner lore:- Seaweed on the shore monsters will roar.

When the sea surfs white monsters will bite.

Watery, Weird and Warty

The best known of all the water monsters is Nessie of Loch Ness in Scotland. She is a dreadful, slimy, slithering Scottish reptile* with a long eel-like neck, enormous jaws and powerful flippers. Nessie emerges from the deep dark dank waters of Loch Ness to prey on American tourists who wear the wrong tartan.

In ancient times this terrible beast would drag foolhardy, hairy Scottish swimmers down into the dark waters of the Loch never to be seen again. However, in 565 St Columba commanded Nessie to be a 'Good Beastie' and thereafter she was, and left the swimmers alone (as far as we know).

In 1934, one moonlit night, a student called Arthur Grant was riding home, when he nearly ran into Nessie on his motorbike as she was crossing the road back to the Loch.

*Possibly a plesiosaur.

Most gigantic of all sea monsters is the Kraken. It is often as much as one and a half miles long and frequently mistaken for an island.

Possibly the squashiest of the water monsters are the 'Globsters', shapeless warty humps of green flesh covered in hair. They are found on Australian beaches and are often called Bruce or Sheila. If they are trodden on they can be very dangerous especially if they go bright red.

There once was a gorilla called King Kong
Who was so very big and strong
He went for a walk and arrived in New York
And caused the most monstrous Ding-Dong!

Movie Monsters 1

Monsters are enthusiastic movie goers. They often go to the cinema to watch themselves on the big screen. They stuff themselves with monster-size buckets of popcorn, suck and slurp ice lollies, and guzzle big cokes. Have you ever sat behind anyone like that?

Movie Monster lore:–*Scrunch, gobble gobble slurp. It all ends in a burp.*

Favourite monster movies are:–

'The Creature from the Black Lagoon'
'The Beast from 1,000 Fathoms'
'The Abominable Snowman'
'The Thing from Outer Space'
'The Other Thing from Outer Space'
'Jaws'
'Alien'
'Godzilla'
'The Blob'

Hollywood has had many famous monster movie stars like King Kong the Giant gorilla. He terrified New York searching for his true love, the fair Fay Wray.

The Blob is a jelly-like monster that blobbed and gobbled everything in its path, becoming bigger and bigger. This film has lots of sticky moments.

I'm just a blob, blob blobbing along

Faster Wilber faster! It's gaining!

I know! I know!

Frankenstein's monster stepping out for two chilli and tuna and cheese and pepperoni take-away pizzas.

Movie Monsters 2

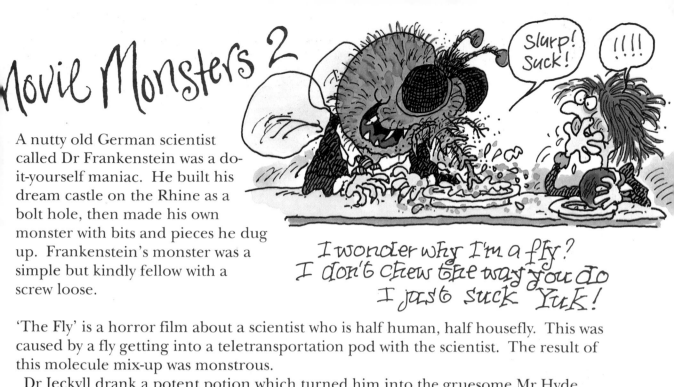

A nutty old German scientist called Dr Frankenstein was a do-it-yourself maniac. He built his dream castle on the Rhine as a bolt hole, then made his own monster with bits and pieces he dug up. Frankenstein's monster was a simple but kindly fellow with a screw loose.

Slurp! Suck!

!!!!

I wonder why I'm a fly? I don't chew the way you do I just suck Yuk!

'The Fly' is a horror film about a scientist who is half human, half housefly. This was caused by a fly getting into a teletransportation pod with the scientist. The result of this molecule mix-up was monstrous.

   Dr Jeckyll drank a potent potion which turned him into the gruesome Mr Hyde. Mr Hyde was a monster with superhuman strength; he could see in the dark, had hairs on his chest, long white teeth and curly hair. Does your mum offer you potent potions and say, 'it'll put hairs on your chest'? Beware.

Heh! Heh! Heh! Heh! Heh! Heh! Heh!

...See old Jeckyll's been mixing his drinks again.

Yah! Bad show, what?

When space monsters glow   it's time to go.

Space Monsters

In 1952 in Virginia, USA, a group of friends investigating a bright flashing light on a hillside, were chased by a huge, floating, glowing space monster with bulging eyes and long tentacle-like fingers.

Space monsters are reported to have visited Earth for thousands of years. In 1961 Joe Simontan of Wisconsin, USA, was visited in his back garden by little green men. They gave him a pancake, and said that it was their mission to seek out New Worlds, to go where no little green men had gone before and to start an Intergalactic Pancake Delivery Service.

Some space monsters are not so friendly. In 1954 a lorry driver in Venezuela stopped in surprise to see a strange unearthly craft hovering over the road. Small, hairy monsters with glowing eyes emerged from the spacecraft and attacked the lorry driver. He was then thrown over four metres through the air. Since then the lorry driver has been wary of the small and hairy.

Stranger than Strange

Heel! Heel! Sheep for tea!

Mon Dieu!

Oh! You bad beast!

mon Dieu!

Mon Dieu!

Deep in the jungles of Madagascar grows a tree with long tendrils covered in sharp spines. Its branches reach out and entwine unsuspecting picnickers, their cheese and tomato sandwiches and their smoky bacon crisps. Once snared, its victims are dragged into its dark heart never to be seen again. Never sit under this tree, it is the 'Man-Eating Tree of Madagascar'.*

*In ancient times Madagascar was known as the Land of the Man-Eating Trees.

In Gevandan, France between the years of 1764 and 1767 the countryside was plagued by a wild beast. It was bright red, covered in scales, with a mouth the size of a lion. It was the terror of the local shepherds, carrying off sheep, tourists and croissants at every opportunity.

Isuchi-Gumo is a Japanese Goblin Spider with the terrifying ability to enlarge its horrible, hairy body at night. Could this be the original Little Miss Muffet?

Gobble Gobble

Eeek! Horwid spidwer!

Monstrous Meals

Monster Menus

~ Breakfast ~

Vile Bile Juice (orange or lemon)
Weetabits (crunchy, wholesome bits of anything)
Cold, lumpy porridge (for the hairy, hardy monster)
Snap, Crackle & Belch (to wake you up in the morning)
Musheli (for the healthy monster) containing dried maggots,
yoghurt coated beetles, dried worms and lice flakes
Boiled Bad Eggs with toasted fingers (dip and crunch)

~ Snacks ~

Blood Oranges
Yeti Yoghurt
Smoky Bogie flavoured crisps

Monsters are greedy gobblers, they believe in making a meal out of every meal time.
They shove enormous quantities of food into their ever open, vast,
dribbling jaws. Monster manners are dreadful.

~ Lunch ~

Snot Sandwiches with granary bread
Giant Giblet Burger (charcoal grilled)
Sliced Snake Salad
Snail and Salad Cream Sandwich
Tripe in warm milk (for the sickly monster)
Hot Thick Sick Soup (for the cold monster)
Croque Monstère

~ High Tea ~

Vomit Vol-Au-Vents
Snottage Rolls
Green Gilbert Gateau
Snail Slime Sponge Cake

~ Dinner ~

Spit Soup
Shepherd Pie (made with three fresh shepherds)
Toad-in-the-hole with mashed maggots
Fried fingers with chips
Hot Potty Pie with Fried Lice
Squashed Fly Pie
Mucus Mousse
Green Mould Jelly with Frozen Eyes Cream

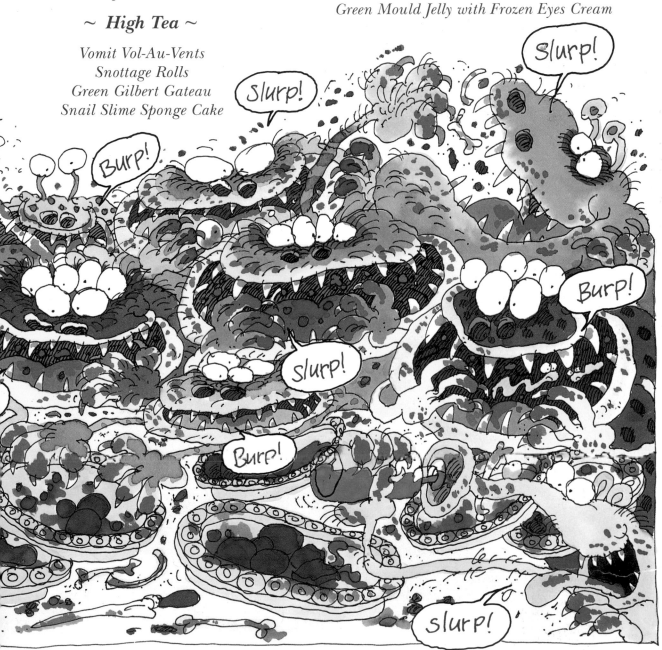

They slurp soup, chew with their mouths open, lick their plates, eat with their paws
and put their elbows on the table. They never say 'please', 'thank you'
or 'excuse me'. And they always burp.

Monsters at Work

Even monsters need to earn an honest crust. Some professions have more monster appeal than others. Many monsters are attracted to teaching.

They often reach the top as headmasters or headmistresses, commanding respect mingled with terror.

You horrible little monster!

Yes, sir.

Get off the grass!!

Park keeping appeals to monsters. It is a healthy out-of-door occupation with plenty of exercise, and the opportunity to meet lots of children.

Eeeeeeek!

Werewolves make dedicated night watchmen. They are physically well suited for this job as they can see in the dark and move silently.

Children who have nannies remember them well after they are grown up. This is not surprising as lots of nannies are monsters. Hairy monsters make super nannies as babies love to cuddle into their hairy chests.

Nanny lore:–

Nanny knows best
You'll get a cold on the chest
Just put on a vest
Nanny knows best.

I love my Nanny, she's so weird.
Especially when she shaves her beard, she really thinks it's such a lark to race me madly round the park.

Monstrous Old Jokes

Monsters love to cackle and titter.
Here are a few old belly laughs and rib-ticklers.

Monster Rhymes

This little monster went to market.
This little monster stayed at home.
This little monster had roast beef.
This little monster had none. And this little monster went wee..wee... all the way home.

Wee...wee...wee...

Aren't I pretty?

Pom! Pom!

Monday's monster's fair of face.
Tuesday's monster's full of grace.

Wednesday's monster's full of woe.

Woe woe woe

I've a long way to go!

Thursday's monster's got far to go.

I love you, have my best bone.

Oh, thank you.

Friday's monster is loving and giving.

Saturday's monster works hard for his living.

It's hard work but I like it.

But the monster that is born on the sabbath day is bonny, blithe*, good and gay.*

I'm so bonny.

I'm so happy.

I'm so good.

Hee! Hee!

*Blithe: Old monster for happy

*Gay: Old monster for gleeful.

It is said that
any monster bits that
are chopped off a monster
will re-form into
a complete monster
again.
You have been warned.

Grrrr!

First published by HarperCollins 1991. First published in Picture Lions 1992
Picture Lions is an imprint of the Children's Division, part of HarperCollins Publishers Limited,
77-85 Fulham Palace Road, Hammersmith, London W6 8JB
Text and illustrations copyright © Colin & Jacqui Hawkins 1991
Printed in Great Britain